The Dream of Little Joseph

José Francisco Huizache Verde

José Francisco Huizache Verde

Copyright © 2018 José Francisco Huizache Verde

All rights reserved.

ISBN-13: 978-1723398209
ISBN-10: 1723398209

ALEJANDRO C. AGUIRRE PUBLISHING/EDITORIAL, CORP.

Copyright © 2018 José Francisco Huizache Verde. Alejandro C. Aguirre Publishing/Editorial, Corp.

All rights reserved. No part of this publication may be reproduced, stored in a retrieval system or transmitted in any form by any means electronic, mechanical, photocopying, recording or otherwise, except brief extracts for the purpose of reviews, without the permission of the publisher and copyright owner.

Printed in the USA

ISBN-13: 978-1723398209

ISBN-10: 1723398209

Número de control de la biblioteca del congreso de E.E.U.U.:

Todos los derechos reservados. Ninguna parte de este libro puede ser reproducida o transmitida de cualquier forma o por cualquier medio, electrónico o mecánico, incluyendo fotocopia, grabación, o por cualquier sistema de almacenamiento y recuperación, sin permiso escrito del propietario del copyright, y sin el previo consentimiento de la editorial, excepto cuando se utilice para elaborar reseñas de la obra, críticas literarias y/o ciertos usos comerciales dispuestos por la ley de copyright.

Las opiniones expresadas en este trabajo son exclusivas del autor y no reflejan necesariamente las opiniones del editor.

Este libro fue impreso en los Estados Unidos de Norteamérica.

Fecha de revisión: 07/21/2018

Para realizar pedidos de este libro, contacte con:

Alejandro C. Aguirre Publishing/Editorial, Corp.

Dentro de EE. UU. al 917.870.0233

Desde México al 01.917.870.0233

Desde otro país al +1.917.870.0233

En México al +52.246.144.9147

Ventas: www.AlejandrocAguirre.com editorial@alejandrocaguirre.com

José Francisco Huizache Verde

DEDICATION

Dedicated to all children of the world, especially to my two children: Lionell and Cassandra.

May God always care and protect them.

Whit a lot of good blessings to the most friendly and Amaising person. For Terri

ACKNOWLEDGE

I thank God for giving me the opportunity to share my project with the world.

Thank you to my beautiful wife for her full support.

To my two mothers Josefina Verde and Rosa Verde, in the same way to my fathers Alfredo Huizache and Erasto León.

Thank you all for your trust!

In a beautiful country, rich in culture and natural scenery, down the Guanajuato Basin,

there was a hidden town where little **Joseph** lived.

He, like many other children, went to elementary school, located in the center of the town which at the time, he was in fifth grade.

It was the year of 1996, and the festivities of the people approached. There were days filled with activities and joy for everyone. For **Joseph**, it was even more special, the festivities were celebrated a month after his birthday.

Joseph was very happy because going back to school meant that his birthday was coming too.

He saw that his friends celebrated their birthdays with candy, clowns and best of all, Cake!
This was what **Joseph** liked best.

This genius boy used to help his mother cook cakes, he knew that one day he would have one for him.

It was very fun to beat dough, scrape oranges, and combine all the ingredients to achieve a work of art of baking.

With his mother, Doña Rosa, **Joseph** made cakes of all kinds, jellies, cheese pies, typical sweets (alfeñiques) and "chocomiles", that's what they called the chocomilk.

But, **Joseph's** favorite cake was a very special and delicious one. It was shaped like a thread, it was filled with delicious fruit with strawberry jam and grated coconut on top.

Hummm! He said while he imagined it when he was going to school.

At the end of the school day, at home, his mother put him to do several things to sell.

In addition to delightful cakes, she also sold at night the delicious "chocomiles" which were very famous because they contained a secret ingredient that only she and **Joseph** knew.

That night, **Joseph** fell exhausted in his bed since he was a boy who loved to help his mom.

He was so tired that he forgot the next day was his birthday.

Thus, he stayed dreaming that it was the perfect day, nothing is greater than a child's birthday, cute toys, funny and entertaining clowns, children's music, beloved friends, fun games, "piñatas", food, and many beautiful things to celebrate and share with the whole family.

Everything was joy, when suddenly, the whole thing went cloudy and there was nothing and nobody, Joseph was alone in some unknown place without being able to shout, hear, and much less to move.

He did not know what was happening. When suddenly, a strong and evil voice called him,

"Joseph, Joseph, Joseph!"

The little one did not know what he would face.

Suddenly in the shadows there appeared a large fat image with yellow eyes like fire and huge wings.

He raised his head as high as he could to visualize a monster in the form of a dragon.

Without fear, surprisingly he shouted:

"Do you know where everyone is?"
And the monster said, "They are my prisoners and you will not see them again".
Joseph remained thinking and asked, "What do you want from me, dragon?"
The monster replied, "I love you and your delicious cakes, they look very tasty!

Ummmmmmmm!"

Then, out of nowhere, appeared a magical gift that shone and illuminated all that darkness, as weapons that would support **Joseph** to defeat the monster.

A very special metal armor that did not weigh and did not break with anything.

It helped **Joseph** to move very fast with a very sharp sword and a strong shield to protect himself from that fearsome dragon.

The monster was surprised and was enraged to see that little **Joseph** got up with courage to fight against him.

So the battle started. The fierce dragon no longer wanted to confine **Joseph** alone, he wanted to eat him because no one had ever faced him before.

José Francisco Huizache Verde

They fought hard and ferociously throughout the night, the monster saw that **Joseph** was not going to give up since he wanted his perfect day again.

When suddenly... Oh! Nooo!

The little warrior is hurt and falls to the ground.

His opponent was about to sing victory, it's the end for **Joseph**.

José Francisco Huizache Verde

The monster exclaimed, "For a moment I thought you would beat me! But you are defeated!"

The monster offered to return everything if he did not give up. Then **Joseph** took one last deep breath as he was already very tired.

As soon as he felt the monster nearby, he turned and struck a blow that would leave the monster unconscious lying on the ground.

When the monster fell, **Joseph** immediately woke up and shook his face from the tears produced by the terrible dream.

He shouted and his mom ran to see what had happened to her little son.

Joseph told her that the monster had eaten his cake. Mom asked him,
"What do you say, honey?"

Then he ran to the kitchen, and by his surprise, there was his big cake.

It has three stories, three milks, filled with fruit and covered with the strawberry jam that he liked so much.
That reminded him of what the dragon said, "I'll return everything if you do not give up."
Suddenly he heard a voice that said, "What is promised is debt, enjoy it!"
Joseph answered, "Thank you!"

And he had the happiest birthday in a long time.

birthday

Joseph

ACTIVITY PAGE

VOCABULARY:

1. Alfeñiques: is a confection molded from sugar paste. The design and construction of these figures can vary from region to region.

2. Chocomiles: is chocolate powder added to hot water while "*Chocomiles*" is the extra milky version of hot chocolate or chocomilk.

3. Piñatas: is a figure, traditionally made from a clay pot covered with paper maché and painted or decorated with brightly colored tissue paper that is filled with candy and fruit or other goodies.

QUESTIONS:

1. What was your favorite part of the story?
2. Who are the characters in the tale?
3. What did you learn from the Dream of little Joseph?

ABOUT AUTHOR

José Francisco Huizache Verde was born in Celaya, Guanajuato, Mexico in a humble cradle of a family with good principles and values.

He studied up to the first semester of University.

He is happily married to his wife Mayra and father of two beautiful children.

He moved to the United States in 2006 and he currently resides in Wheeling, Illinois.

Today, he is dedicated to helping people of all ages through his inspiring writings from the depths of his being.

His personal philosophy is: "Give love to all human beings and to provide them with support".

To order this book, contact:

Alejandro C. Aguirre Publishing/Editorial, Corp.

United States: 917.870.0233

Mexico: 01.917.870.0233

Other countries: +1.917.970.0233

In Mexico +52.246.144.9147

Visit: www.AlejandrocAguirre.com editorial@alejandrocaguirre.com

Made in the USA
Lexington, KY
15 August 2018